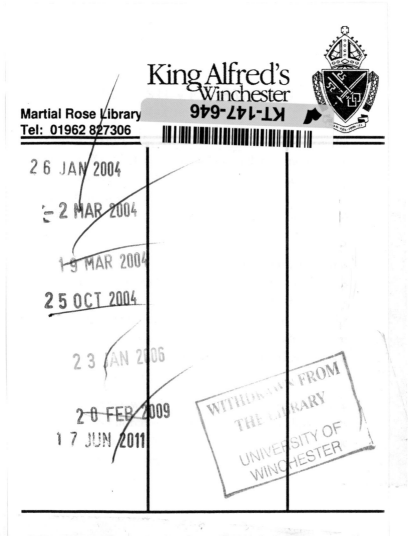

King Alfred's
Winchester

OXFORD BOOKWORMS LIBRARY
Thriller & Adventure

The Silver Sword

Stage 4 (1400 headwords)

Series Editor: Jennifer Bassett
Founder Editor: Tricia Hedge
Activities Editors: Jennifer Bassett and Alison Baxter

IAN SERRAILLIER

The Silver Sword

Retold by
John Escott

Illustrated by
Martin McKenna

OXFORD UNIVERSITY PRESS

Oxford University Press

Great Clarendon Street, Oxford OX2 6DP

Oxford New York

Athens Auckland Bangkok Bogotá Buenos Aires Cape Town
Chennai Dar es Salaam Delhi Florence Hong Kong Istanbul Karachi
Kolkata Kuala Lumpur Madrid Melbourne Mexico City Mumbai Nairobi
Paris São Paulo Shanghai Singapore Taipei Tokyo Toronto Warsaw
with associated companies in
Berlin Ibadan

OXFORD and OXFORD ENGLISH
are trade marks of Oxford University Press

ISBN 0 19 423045 7

Original edition © Ian Serraillier 1956
First published by Jonathan Cape Ltd 1956
This simplified edition © Oxford University Press 2000

Third impression 2001

First published in Oxford Bookworms 1995
This second edition published in the Oxford Bookworms Library 2000

Map by Martin Ursell

Typeset by Wyvern Typesetting Ltd, Bristol
Printed in Spain by Unigraf s.l.

CONTENTS

1
The escape

This is a story of a Polish family, and what happened to them during the Second World War, and immediately afterwards. Their home was in Warsaw, and the father, Joseph Balicki, was the headmaster of a school. He and his Swiss wife, Margrit, had three children. In 1940, when the Nazis took Joseph away to prison, Ruth was nearly thirteen, Edek was eleven, and Bronia was three.

Joseph Balicki was sent to a prison in the mountains of South Poland. It was crowded with prisoners, but not many were strong enough to escape. Some did escape, but most of them were caught and brought back, and the others died from the cold in the mountains.

During the first winter, Joseph was too ill to try to escape. He sat looking at the three or four photos of his family that he was allowed to keep, and wondered what was happening to them now.

During the summer his health got better, but now there were more guards. A group of six prisoners tried to escape, and Joseph was one of them. But they were soon caught and brought back, and Joseph was locked in a room alone for a month.

The next winter he was ill again. He still wanted to escape, but he decided to wait until early spring when there would be less snow on the mountains. Very carefully, he made his plans.

He decided to pretend to be a guard. If he did this, he could walk out with the other guards, past the guard-house and through the gate to freedom. But how could he get a guard's uniform?

One morning in March, Joseph made a little ball of paper and threw it at a guard. It hit him behind the ear and made him turn round. The next ball hit the guard on the nose. For this, Joseph was again locked away in a room alone.

Twice each day, a guard brought him food. It was put through a special hole in the door. On the evening of the third day, the guard came with Joseph's food and began to unlock the cover over the hole in the door. In a moment, the guard would look through the hole before putting the food through. Joseph was waiting for this. He had a catapult which was made from sticks, and from the elastic in the sides of his boots. And he had a smooth round stone.

Suddenly, the guard's face appeared at the hole in the door. Joseph shot the stone from the catapult. It hit the guard on the head and knocked him down.

Joseph shot the stone from the catapult.

Now Joseph had to move quickly. Under his bed was a long piece of a blanket, with a bent nail tied to the end of it. Joseph pushed the piece of blanket through the hole in the door. The guard's keys were on the floor, and it took several desperate moments before Joseph managed to pick up the keys with the bent nail and pull them up towards him.

He unlocked his door and pulled the guard inside. Quickly, he took off the guard's uniform and put it on himself. The warm hat covered his ears and helped to hide his face. Then, locking the guard in the room, he hurried outside into the cold and followed the other guards towards the gate. He had watched the guards leaving a hundred times and knew exactly what to do.

'Anything to report?' the officer at the gate asked each guard.

'Nothing, Sir,' they answered.

'Nothing, Sir,' Joseph answered in his best German.

Then he followed the others out of the gate.

He was free!

2
Journey through the air

The village of Zakyna was a kilometre below the prison camp. There was no moon that night, but Joseph could see lights in the windows of the houses. Just below the last houses in the village, the road turned away from the cliff edge. A mail car was stopped with its lights on and its engine going. There was some luggage in the road, and an angry group of people around it.

'You're two hours late!' someone shouted.

'I told you, the snow is making the road dangerous,' replied the driver.

Joseph hid behind the wall of snow at the side of the road. He was on the edge of a cliff, which dropped steeply into the darkness. He heard the sound of large boxes being dropped on to the road.

Joseph moved quietly along the edge of the cliff, and saw a square shape next to the road. In the dark it looked like a cart without wheels. Quickly, he hid underneath.

Suddenly, a heavy box banged down on the boards above his head. He heard boots moving on the wood and in the snow, and the voices of soldiers giving orders. More boxes were put in, and then covered with a heavy cloth. When the soldiers were back in the road, Joseph pulled himself over the wooden side and under the cloth.

A loud voice shouted, 'Are you ready?'

Then somebody answered from the other side of the dark valley, and suddenly the wooden boards Joseph was lying on began to move. They were sliding out into the darkness, away from the road. Where was he?

Joseph lifted the cloth and looked out. He was in a luggage lift, moving through the air!

There were lots of luggage lifts in the mountains. They were driven by electricity and were used for carrying things from one side of a steep valley to the other. Joseph looked

Joseph lifted the cloth and looked out.

ahead into the darkness. Were there soldiers on the other side of the valley, too? If there were, what was he going to do? He could not get away unseen, and he had no gun.

Then he decided what to do.

At last the lift stopped with a bang, and a light was shining in his face.

'I have a gun,' Joseph said calmly. 'If you make a sound, I'll shoot you.'

An angry Polish voice said something.

'Be quiet, or I'll shoot,' Joseph said. 'Give me your light.'

He took the light from the shaking hands and turned it on the other face. The man had a grey beard, and a rough farmer's face. Joseph felt better. The man was Polish, like himself.

Joseph spoke more gently. 'Take out the boxes. Is the lift worked from this end? Good. Then we shan't have visitors from the other side.'

The man put the boxes into a shed, near the lift. Then he took one for himself and carried it to his house. Joseph followed him. The box contained food and clothing from the town.

An old woman was waiting inside the house, and she looked frightened when she saw Joseph. He threw his hat and coat on to a chair.

'Here's my gun,' he said with a smile. 'It's a bar of chocolate.' He broke it into three pieces and gave them some.

'I don't understand,' said the man slowly. 'You speak and look like a Pole, but your uniform—'

Just then, they heard a bell ringing on the other side of the valley.

'That's the prison bell,' said the man. 'They ring it when a prisoner escapes.'

'I am the prisoner,' Joseph told them.

The next day, some German soldiers came to the house, looking for the escaped prisoner, but Joseph hid in the chimney until they had gone.

He stayed with the Polish couple for two weeks. They were kind people and they looked after him well. His thin body became stronger, and he began to look quite healthy. But on the fifteenth day he left. The old man guided him through the mountains for three days, then he said goodbye.

And so Joseph began the first part of his long journey home.

3
The silver sword

It took Joseph four and a half weeks to walk home to Warsaw. He knew the city well, but now there was almost no street that he recognized, and not an undamaged building anywhere. People were making their homes in cellars, or in caves which they had made in the ruined buildings. The only busy place was the railway, where trains moved through day and night, carrying soldiers to Russia or bringing back the injured from Germany.

It was three days before Joseph found the street where he used to live. The school and his house had disappeared.

'What happened?' he asked people, but most of them were new and not able to help him. Then he saw Mrs Krause, the mother of a child who had been at his school.

'The Nazis destroyed your school,' she said.

'What happened to my wife?'

'They came for her in January last year, during the night. She's in Germany, probably working on the land.'

'Did the children go with her?' asked Joseph.

Mrs Krause turned away. 'I don't know anything about them,' she said.

But Joseph knew she was hiding bad news. 'Tell me, please,' he said.

So she told him all she knew. 'On the night your wife was taken away, somebody shot at the car. One of the Nazi soldiers was hit in the arm before they got away. But an hour later, a lot more soldiers came back and destroyed the house with a bomb. The children have not been seen since.'

That was all Mrs Krause could tell Joseph, but he knew that she thought the children were dead.

For several days, Joseph searched the city for his children. At night he returned home to the Krauses, who gave him food and a bed.

One night, Mrs Krause said, 'You can't go on like this. Almost certainly your children died when the bomb went off. Search for your wife instead of them.'

'Germany is a large place,' said Joseph. 'How will I find her?'

'Perhaps she escaped, like you,' said Mrs Krause. 'Did you decide to meet somewhere if you were separated?'

'Yes, we did. In Switzerland. My wife is Swiss and her parents still live there.'

Mrs Krause smiled. 'Then go to Switzerland, and perhaps you will find her there.'

But Joseph spent several more days looking for his children. One afternoon, he was searching among the ruins of his old home when he found a small silver sword. It was about fourteen centimetres long, with a dragon at one end. It was a paper knife, used for opening letters. Joseph had once given it to his wife for a birthday present.

While he was cleaning the knife, he saw a small boy watching him. The boy was thin and his clothes were old and dirty. He was carrying a wooden box under one arm, and a small grey cat under the other.

'Give me that sword,' said the boy.

'But it's mine,' said Joseph.

'You found it here, and this is my place.'

Joseph explained about his house.

'I'll give you food for it,' said the boy, and he offered Joseph a sandwich.

'I have plenty of food,' said Joseph. He put his hand into his pocket, but it was empty. 'That's *my* sandwich!' he laughed. 'You took it from my pocket!'

But before Joseph could take it back, the boy ate most of it and gave the rest to his cat.

After a minute, Joseph said, 'I'm looking for my children.

'Give me that sword,' said the boy.

Ruth is fifteen now, and she's tall with fair hair. Edek is thirteen, and Bronia is five.'

'Warsaw is full of children,' said the boy. 'They're all dirty and hungry and they all look alike.'

'I'll give you this sword if you do something for me,' said Joseph. 'If you ever see Ruth or Edek or Bronia, you must tell them about our meeting. Tell them I'm going to Switzerland to find their mother. Tell them to follow me as soon as they can.'

The boy took the sword and put it in his wooden box.

'I'm starting the journey to Switzerland tonight,' said Joseph. 'I'm going to hide on a train. Where's the best place to jump on a train unseen?'

'You will be caught and shot,' said the boy. 'Or you will die from the cold.'

'I still have to go,' said Joseph.

'Meet me tonight, when it's dark, and I'll show you the place where the trains slow down,' said the boy.

That night, when it was dark, Joseph said goodbye to the Krauses and left their house for the last time. The boy was waiting for him at the bottom of the street.

'We must use the back streets,' said the boy. 'If the Nazi soldiers see us, they'll shoot.'

'What's that you're carrying?' said Joseph.

'Bread,' said the boy. 'I borrowed it from the Nazi soldiers. They have plenty of it. Take it, you'll be hungry.'

'I've a lot to thank you for,' said Joseph, as they waited beside the railway. 'What's your name?'

The boy said nothing. He sat holding his cat and the wooden box.

'Will you come with me?' asked Joseph.

The boy didn't answer the question. He opened the wooden box and took out the silver sword. 'This will bring me luck, and it will bring you luck because you gave it to me. I don't tell anybody my name – it's not safe. But I'll tell you because you gave me the sword.' He whispered. 'It's Jan.'

A train was coming.

'Goodbye, Jan,' said Joseph. 'Remember your promise. Whatever happens, I shall not forget you.'

It was dark, and Jan did not see him jump on to the train. It was raining heavily now, and Jan hurried back into the dark streets, with the grey cat inside his coat. The wooden box was under his arm.

And he thought of the silver sword inside.

4
The children

What happened to Joseph's family that night over a year ago? Was Mrs Krause's story true? Did the Nazi soldiers take Joseph's wife away? Did they return and blow up the house with the children in it?

This is what happened.

It was snowing that night in Warsaw. Ruth and Bronia were asleep in the room next to their mother's bedroom. Edek's room was on the top floor. He was asleep when the Nazi soldiers came, but woke up when he heard a noise outside his door.

The door was locked. Edek shouted and banged on it, but could not get out. He listened. In his mother's room, the men were giving orders, but Edek could not hear what they were saying. In the ceiling was a small square door that led to the attic. There was a ladder between his bed and the wall. Quietly, he moved it under the square door and climbed up.

There was a rifle hidden in the attic, and Edek took it and climbed back down to his room. The noises in the room below had stopped. He looked out into the street and saw a car waiting outside the front door. Two Nazi soldiers were pulling his mother towards it.

He opened the window. He was afraid to shoot until his mother was safely in the car. His first shot hit a soldier's arm. The man shouted with pain and jumped in beside the driver. Edek aimed the next two shots at the car wheels. He hit one, but the car got away.

Edek used the rifle to break down his bedroom door, then he did the same to the door of his sisters' room. Bronia was crying and Ruth was trying to calm her.

'I hit one of them,' said Edek.

'That was silly,' said Ruth. 'They'll come back for us now. We must get away from here before they do.'

Ruth dressed Bronia while Edek fetched overcoats and boots and warm caps. Ruth pulled a coat on over her nightdress, and put a scarf round Bronia.

'We can't go out the front way. I can hear another car coming,' said Edek. 'And the back wall is too high and there are soldiers in that street. We'll have to go over the roof.'

He picked up Bronia and led the way upstairs. He was wearing his father's thick overcoat and carrying the rifle on his back.

When they were in the attic, Edek broke the window to the roof and climbed out into the cold night. Ruth lifted Bronia up to him, then followed her.

14

'Listen, Bronia,' said Edek. 'If you make a sound, we shall all be killed. Walk behind me and hold on to the rifle. And don't look down!'

The roof was steep, and the snow made it difficult to stand or walk. Edek managed to climb across to the chimney, with Bronia holding on to the rifle behind him.

'Walk behind me and hold on to the rifle,' said Edek.

She was too afraid to speak or make a noise. Then he reached back and pulled Ruth up after him. They could not see what was happening in the street, but they could hear shouting and the sound of cars stopping suddenly.

The houses in this street were joined together, and so they were able to move from roof to roof and get away. They had gone a hundred metres when the first bomb exploded. Fire lit up the sky above their home, and they fell flat in the snow. The roof shook and the whole city seemed to tremble. Another bomb exploded, and smoke and flames came from the windows.

'Hurry,' said Edek. 'We won't let them get us now.'

They moved quickly across the roof-tops until they found a fire escape on the outside of a building, then they went down to the street. On they ran, not knowing or caring where they went as long as they left the terrible flames behind them.

It was the beginning of another grey winter's day before they finally stopped at a ruin of a bombed house. They slept inside it until the early afternoon, then woke up cold and hungry.

They made their new home in a cellar at the other end of the city. When they asked the Polish Council about their mother, they were told she had been taken to Germany to work on the land. Nobody knew which part of Germany.

'The war will end soon,' they were told, 'and your mother will come back.'

They quickly made their new home as comfortable as they could. Edek got a mattress and some curtains from a bombed building. He gave the mattress to Ruth and Bronia. The curtains made good sheets. He stole blankets from a Nazi camp, one for each of them. Here they lived for the rest of that winter and the spring.

Food was not easy to find. Except when Edek found work for a few days, there was no money to buy any. Sometimes they begged for it, other times they stole it from the Nazis. They saw nothing wrong in stealing from their enemies, but they were careful never to steal from their own people.

Edek got a mattress and some curtains from a bombed building.

Edek kept himself busy, but Ruth found her new life difficult. Then she started a school. She invited other lost children, of Bronia's age and a little older. While Edek was out finding food, she told them stories, and taught them to read and write. There was soon a crowd of poor, homeless children wanting to join her school, but there was only room for twelve.

In the early summer, they went to live in the forest outside the city. Life was healthier here, and there were plenty of other families for the children to play with. Ruth's school sometimes had as many as twenty-five children in it.

Because of the kindness of the farmers, it was easier to get food. The farmers were not allowed to sell food to anyone except the Nazis, but they gave the children whatever they could. And they also hid food in cellars or holes in the ground. Then the children helped them to take it secretly into the towns, to sell to the Polish people.

Edek was one of the children who did this. He went off to the town at night with butter sewn into his coat, or hidden among wood in a cart. But one night, Edek did not return. Ruth questioned other families in the forest, but no one had seen him. After some days, she discovered that he had called at a house in a village. The secret police had been there, searching for hidden food. They discovered the butter that was sewn into Edek's coat. After setting fire to the house, they had taken the owner and Edek away.

'From now on,' Ruth told Bronia, 'we will have to look after ourselves.'

5
Jan and Ivan

Two years passed without news of Edek. Ruth and Bronia returned to Warsaw each winter, and went back to the forest in the summer. But in the summer of 1944, the skies were full of planes, and they could hear bombs falling in the city. Though the children did not know it, the Russian army was moving west and the battle for Warsaw was beginning.

By January 1945, the Nazis were gone and the city was in the control of the Russians. That winter, Ruth and Bronia had waited in the forest because of the fighting, but now they came back into the city. The Warsaw that they had known had disappeared. Bombs had destroyed the buildings, and there were no streets left.

Somehow, they found the cellar which had been their home for two years. The chairs and beds had gone, but they had brought their blankets from the forest. Then some boys in Ruth's school mended the table and made chairs from boxes, and lessons began again.

One day, Bronia came running into the cellar. 'There's a boy lying down outside and I don't think he can get up,' she said. 'I've never seen him before.'

The boy was lying on some stones. Ruth thought he might be any age between nine and thirteen. His face was thin and white and his eyes were closed. A thin cockerel stood beside the boy's head, making noises at anyone who

A thin cockerel stood beside the boy's head.

went near him. Ruth chased the cockerel away.

'Does anyone know him?' she asked the children.

Nobody did.

'He looks ill from hunger,' said Ruth. 'Yankel, will you help me lift him down to the cellar? Eva, find him something to eat, some soup if you can get it.'

They carried the boy down to the cellar and, after a few minutes, he opened his eyes.

'Where's Jimpy?' he said.

Suddenly, the cockerel appeared in a hole in the wall and jumped down beside the boy.

'Jimpy, Jimpy!' cried the boy, and reached out towards the bird.

'What's your name?' asked Ruth.

'Won't tell you,' said the boy.

'Look, Eva's brought you some soup,' said Ruth. 'You'll feel better in a minute. Sit up and drink it.'

A girl pushed through the crowd at the door. She had a small wooden box in her hand. 'I found this in the street,' she said. 'I think it's his.'

'Give it to him,' said Ruth.

The boy took the box and smiled. Everyone wanted to look inside, but he wouldn't open it. But he told them his name. It was Jan.

For some days, Jan was too ill to leave. Then, when he was better, he didn't want to go. So he made his home with Ruth and Bronia, and became one of the family. He carried the box everywhere, but he never opened it.

Several streets away a new Russian guard hut had appeared. One afternoon, Ruth went there. 'I want to see your officer,' she said to the guard standing outside.

'The whole of Warsaw wants to see my officer,' said the guard. 'Run away and play, little girl.'

'I'm not a little girl,' said Ruth. 'I'll be eighteen next week.'

The guard smiled. 'Well, because it's your birthday next week, I'll ask him.' He went into the hut, then came out a few moments later. 'My officer says come back the year after next.'

But before he could stop her, Ruth pushed past him into the hut. Inside, an officer sat behind a desk.

'Come out!' shouted the guard.

'All right, Ivan,' said the officer. 'I'll talk to her.' He looked at Ruth. 'What do you want?'

21

Ruth pushed past the guard into the hut.

'I want food and clothes and blankets, pencils and paper. I've got sixteen children—'

The surprised officer nearly fell off his chair.

'Seventeen, if you count my brother, Edek, who is lost,' went on Ruth. 'Bronia is my sister, and the others are children at my school. They are all half dead from hunger, but they want to learn and have nothing to write on. And I want you to find Edek. He's been lost for two years.'

The officer waved some papers at her. 'See these? They contain information about missing people, about ten to each page. But it's an impossible job. Perhaps I'll burn the lot!'

'Don't do that,' said Ruth. 'The writing is only on one side of the paper. We can use the back of it at my school for writing on.'

The officer laughed, and Ruth laughed, too.

'I'll take the information about your brother,' he said. 'But I warn you, nothing will happen.'

'Thank you,' said Ruth.

'Come back tomorrow,' said the officer.

She came back the next day and the guard, Ivan, was waiting for her. He had sugar, bread and six blankets to give her.

'Sign your name,' he said. 'And put your address.'

She wrote 'Bombed cellar' and told him where it was.

A week later, Ruth was preparing a birthday tea. Most of the children had been invited. Suddenly, she heard a noise and ran outside to find Jan fighting with a soldier. The knife in Jan's hand was near the soldier's neck, and Jimpy the cockerel was biting the soldier's ankles.

'Jan, drop that knife!' she cried. She threw herself into the fight and they all fell on to the ground. Ruth knocked the knife from Jan's hand.

'That's a nice welcome, isn't it?' said Ivan the guard, as he picked up his cap and brushed dust off it.

Ruth picked up the knife. 'Don't you understand, Jan?'

she said. 'They're our friends.'

'They're soldiers,' said Jan.

'They're Russian soldiers, not Nazis. They've come to make us free and to look after us.'

'I hate all soldiers,' said Jan. And he wouldn't come back into the cellar when the others went inside.

'I've some information about your brother, Edek,' Ivan told Ruth. 'He's in a camp in Posen.'

Ruth threw her arms round his neck and kissed him. 'Thank you, thank you!'

'And I've brought a birthday present for you,' he said. 'It's some chocolate.'

'What's chocolate?' said Bronia.

Suddenly, Jan appeared at the door. He was crying.

'Don't cry, boy,' said Ivan. 'I'm not angry.'

Jan was holding out his little wooden box. It was in pieces. 'You fell on it and broke it!' he cried.

'I'll mend it for you,' said Ivan.

Jan shook his head angrily, and something fell from the broken box. It was the silver sword that Joseph had given him more than two years before.

It was the silver sword.

24

Ruth picked it up and looked closely at it. Where had she seen it before? Then she recognized it. It was the birthday present her father had given to her mother before the war. Then she, too, began to cry.

'More tears!' said Ivan. 'Excuse me, while I go outside and fetch my umbrella!'

And he went away wondering what it was all about.

6
Looking for Edek

While Bronia was asleep that night, Ruth and Jan talked. There was a lot Ruth wanted to know about her father, and Jan told her the little that he remembered.

'Why didn't you speak about him before?' Ruth wanted to know. 'Surely he told you our names?'

But war does strange things to young people. The worry of finding food and staying alive each day was enough to make Jan forget Joseph. But now he remembered him. And he remembered something else.

'He was going to Switzerland to find your mother,' said Jan.

By the morning, Ruth knew what she must do.

'We're going to Switzerland to find Father and Mother,' she told Bronia.

'Where's that?' asked Bronia.

'Millions of kilometres away,' said Jan.

'Spring is coming,' said Ruth, 'and in summer it will be

lovely sleeping under the stars. We'll go to Posen first, to find Edek. It's only two hundred kilometres. We can beg for food.'

'I'll steal it,' said Jan.

Ivan brought them shoes to wear, and a wooden box which he had made for Jan. They left Warsaw carrying enough food for a day, two blankets, Jimpy the cockerel, and the wooden box with the sword in it.

The road out of the city was crowded with refugees. Some were going one way, some the other – it didn't seem to matter which way as long as they were moving. Lorries full of soldiers went past them.

'I wish we could ride on a lorry,' said Jan. 'Jimpy's tired of me carrying him and he doesn't like walking.'

'I like walking,' said Bronia. She was proud of her shoes. Not many of the refugees wore shoes.

But she became tired later and was glad when a lorry stopped and let them ride for a while. They sat in the back and ate the food which they had brought in their pockets. It was evening when the lorry stopped for them to get down, a hundred and sixty kilometres nearer Posen.

That night, they slept in an empty barn. But no lorries stopped the next day, and by evening they had only walked thirty kilometres. Their feet hurt and they were very tired.

On the afternoon of the fourth day, they arrived at Posen. At the first guard hut, Ruth showed a soldier the piece of paper which Ivan had given her. It had Edek's name and address on it.

Lorries full of soldiers went past them.

'The camp is a large building, down by the river,' the guard told them. And they went to find it.

The secretary at the camp knew nothing about Edek, but a doctor was able to help them.

'I sent Edek Balicki to the Warthe camp with the other sick prisoners,' he said. Before Ruth could ask about Edek's illness, he was gone.

'The camp is only a kilometre away, down the river,' said the secretary.

But Edek was not at the Warthe camp either. The man who spoke to Ruth remembered him well.

'He was a wild boy,' he said. 'He ran away this morning, but I don't know where he went.'

Ruth did not want to go on to Switzerland without Edek. In the village of Kolina, just north of Posen, there was a large field kitchen, so it was there that the three children went next. Everyone else seemed to be going there, and they soon became part of the moving crowd.

At the village, Ruth, Bronia and Jan were put in a field with a lot of other young people, then later told to join a queue for dinner. Ruth could smell soup as the line of hungry children moved towards the Russian field kitchens.

'Cheer up, the war is almost over,' said the cook, as he put soup into a bowl and gave it to Jan. He saw the cockerel under Jan's arm and put an extra spoonful of soup into the bowl. 'That's for your sick friend,' he told Jan. 'Let's hope it makes him sit up and sing!'

Someone put bread into Jan's hand and he moved on

past the kitchens to find a corner to sit down.

'Look where you're going!' a voice shouted.

Jan fell over someone's foot. The bowl hit a stone and broke, and the soup ran into the dust. Little bits of meat and bread and vegetables lay on the ground.

Suddenly, all control disappeared. The queue became a group of wild, hungry, fighting children, and Jan was at the centre of the fight as the children tried to get the food. Ruth ran forward, afraid that Bronia would get hurt. She did not know that the cook had picked Bronia up and held her high up out of danger. Ruth, too, became part of the fighting. Children were beneath her and on top of her. She reached for the food – but found a hand. For some reason, she held on to it.

At last the fighting stopped, and the children began to move away. A dirty and bruised Jan stood up, leaving the broken bowl on the ground.

Jimpy lay quite still. His neck was broken.

Ruth was still holding the hand. She looked to see whose hand it was.

It was Edek's.

7
Across the country

There were still a few trains running from Posen, and Ruth, Edek, Bronia and Jan managed to get on one. It was full of refugees and on its way to Berlin. They were in one of the open trucks, which was cold but not so crowded.

'I don't like riding in this truck,' said Bronia.

'We're lucky to be here at all,' Ruth told her. 'Hundreds of people were left behind at Posen, and they may have to wait for weeks.'

'Edek's doctor wanted to send him back to the Warthe camp,' said Jan.

'He said he wanted to make Edek fat,' laughed Bronia. 'Like a chicken for Christmas!'

Ruth looked at her brother. His face was white and very thin. He was sixteen now, and it was two and a half years since she had last seen him, but he did not look like the Edek she remembered.

She looked at Jan. He had helped her with Bronia and kept his sadness to himself after Jimpy's death, but she was not sure that he felt comfortable with Edek.

'Jan may get jealous of Edek,' thought Ruth.

Her fears seemed to come true later when the people in the open truck began to tell of their adventures, and their escapes from the Nazis. After several other stories, Edek told his.

'I was taken to work on a farm near Guben,' he said. 'I tried to run away, but they always caught me – until last winter when the war began to turn against the Nazis. I hid under a train, holding on with my arms and legs, and managed to get back to Poland.'

Jan gave a cruel laugh. 'Why don't you travel that way here? Then the rest of us will have more room.'

'I could never do that again,' said Edek.

'No,' said Jan, looking at Edek's thin arms. 'And you didn't do it before. There's no room to lie under a train, and there's nothing to hold on to.'

Edek pulled Jan to his feet. 'Have you ever looked under a train?' He described the underside of a train in accurate detail, and everyone except Jan believed him.

Edek pulled Jan to his feet.

31

'Why weren't you shaken off?' Jan wanted to know.

'Because the train went through some water, and it began to freeze on me,' said Edek. 'I soon became a piece of ice, frozen to the bottom of the train. Later, I heard Polish voices and knew that we were out of Germany. My voice was the only part of me that wasn't frozen, so I shouted for help. The station master came and broke the ice and carried me out from under the train. It took two hours for the ice to disappear.'

Later, when all was quiet and the refugees lay sleeping under the cold stars, Ruth whispered to Edek, 'Was it really true?'

'Yes, it was true,' he said.

She took his hand and held it in hers. 'Nothing like that must ever happen to you again,' she said.

Nine days later, at the end of May, the train reached Berlin. Some of the refugees immediately disappeared into the dusty ruins of the city, others waited with their luggage, hoping that someone would give them food or tell them where to go. But theirs was the second refugee train that day and there was not enough food for everyone.

But the children were happy. They left the station laughing and shouting, on their way to a refugee camp not far away. Only a few weeks ago, they had been in Warsaw; ten days ago, Edek had been missing. But now they were all together and a third of the way to Switzerland.

The camp was an old, empty cinema. It was warm and

dry and comfortable, and there was food to eat. After four bowls of soup each, the children were given blankets and mattresses and taken to a corner of the hall where they found a place to sleep. But comfortable though it was, the camp was to be their home for only a few days.

'Switzerland is still a long way away,' Ruth reminded the others. 'We must go on.'

'Take the Potsdam road and follow your noses,' the family were told, and off they went, singing a happy song. Russian soldiers marched past them, then lines of women and girls in grey-green uniforms. These were followed by hundreds of carts, pulled by horses.

Next day, the children went across the country towards Bitterfeld and Halle. A British officer had given them some money for food, but this was soon gone and they had to find work to get more. This was difficult because the factories were closed, and the farms were using the freed prisoners of war. Some villages refused to let the children enter because there was no more food or places to stay for refugees.

One camp had a school for Polish children. If they remained there, the children were told, they would receive all the food and schooling and medicine they needed. Edek was very tired when they arrived, and Ruth was ready to stay for as long as he needed to rest. But Edek felt better after a few days, and one look at the silver sword was enough to make him want to go on to Switzerland.

So they came to the edge of the Russian zone.

In the first days of peace after the war ended, there were

many places where it was quite easy to move unnoticed from one zone to another. The children did this somewhere in the Thuringian forest. It was only the different uniforms of the soldiers, and the strange words on the signs, that told them they were now in the American zone.

8
Trouble with a train

It was now the middle of June, and Edek was no better. Each day he walked more slowly, and at night his cough kept Ruth awake. She decided he must rest for a week.

They made a camp near a river and planned to stay there until Ruth and Jan earned enough money to buy Edek a pair of new boots. Ruth took a cleaning job at the local school, and Jan got work on a farm. Edek rested under the trees with Bronia to look after him.

There was plenty of food from the army food kitchens near their camp, but several times Jan came home with tins of meat or fish.

'Where did they come from?' Ruth asked him.

'The farmer,' replied Jan. 'He's very generous.'

But there was strange writing on the tins, and Ruth began to suspect that Jan was lying. 'It's American food, and I know he's stealing it,' she told Edek.

Edek wanted an answer to the mystery. Without saying anything to Ruth, the next afternoon he went alone to the farm where Jan worked. He hid behind a tree and waited.

He saw Jan leave the farm before the day's work was over. Instead of returning to the camp, Jan hurried off the opposite way, and through the town.

Edek followed him to a railway line, where a boy jumped from behind a tree at the side of the road. He waved to Jan, who went across to him.

Edek went closer, but stayed out of sight and waited. He waited so long that he began to wonder if they had gone. Then suddenly Jan came out from behind the trees and ran along one side of the railway, towards the signal ramp. The other boy had disappeared.

Jan came out from behind the trees and
ran towards the signal ramp.

35

Edek climbed into a tree which gave him a good view of the line. He saw Jan climb the signal ramp, which went right across the line, and then lie down flat on the top, above the line. What was he going to do?

'I must go and find out,' thought Edek.

He jumped down from the tree and went to the bottom of the signal ramp.

'What are you doing, Jan?' he called.

Jan did not see Edek until that moment. 'Go away!' he said, angrily.

Then came a noise as the signal changed to green.

'Go away!' Jan screamed at Edek. And he threw himself at the signal and began to pull it.

Edek heard the sound of a distant train.

'Come down!' he shouted to Jan.

Jan took no notice. He worked quickly with a spanner and a pair of wire cutters. The noise of the train grew louder, and dirty smoke rose above the trees.

'There's going to be an accident!' Edek thought, and began to climb up the side of the ramp.

Edek was not strong. Coughing badly, he pulled himself up the ramp to the top. The signal had now changed to red. An angry Jan moved past Edek's face, nearly knocking him off the ramp. He said something, but Edek could not hear him because of the noise of the train. Still worried about an accident, Edek stood up on the ramp and waved at the train. But the signal was at red, where Jan had put it, and the train was already stopping.

Jan worked quickly with a spanner and a pair of wire cutters.

A dark cloud of dirty smoke surrounded Edek. When he finished coughing and wiping the smoke from his eyes, he saw someone shouting at him from below.

It was an American soldier.

And the soldier had a gun in his hand.

Captain Greenwood of the American Army sat in the court-room and looked at the boy in front of him.

'You stopped the train and were going to steal food from it,' he said.

'No,' said Edek. 'I mean, yes, I stopped the train. But no, I wasn't going to steal from it.'

'Why did you do it?' Captain Greenwood did not understand. The boy was ill, and he did not seem the kind of person to play dangerous games with trains.

Before Edek could answer, there was a noise at the back of the court-room. A soldier came forward with a message for Captain Greenwood. There was a whispered conversation, then the captain said, 'Yes, all right. If they can help us, bring them in.'

Ruth, Jan and Bronia were brought in and made to stand beside Edek. Bronia held Ruth's hand and smiled. Jan was biting his lip, but his eyes were angry.

'There's been a mistake, and I've come to explain,' said Ruth in Polish. 'This is Jan. It's all his fault. I want to speak for him.' There was an American soldier who spoke Polish standing near them, and he told Captain Greenwood what Ruth was saying.

'Who is the other child?' asked the captain.

'My sister, Bronia,' said Ruth. 'She has nothing to do with this. We're on our way to Switzerland and we're camping near the river.'

'Have you any parents?' Captain Greenwood asked Jan.

'No, Ruth is my mother now,' said Jan.

Ruth did her best to explain this, and the things that had happened at the railway line.

'So,' Captain Greenwood said to Jan, after Ruth stopped speaking, 'you have no parents. Ruth Balicki is acting as your mother. You say that Edek Balicki did not stop the train, but that you did. Is that right?'

Jan's answer was to make a sudden run for the door. Two guards brought him back, kicking and biting.

'Can *you* control the boy?' Captain Greenwood asked Ruth.

'He's afraid of soldiers,' said Ruth. 'If you send those guards outside, sir, I think he'll behave himself.'

Captain Greenwood was surprised, but he decided to see if the girl was right. 'Leave the boy and wait outside,' he told the guards.

After the soldiers left the room, Jan became calm.

'Tell us what happened,' said Captain Greenwood.

'It wasn't Edek's fault,' Jan said after a moment or two. 'I changed the signal and he came to stop me. I ran away and he was caught. It was easy to get away, but he's a very stupid boy for his age.'

'Why did you stop the train?' said the captain.

'Because of the food trucks.'

'You were going to steal from them yourself?'

'No,' said Jan.

'So you were one of several thieves,' said the captain. 'Was Edek Balicki one, too?'

'No.'

'Who are the others?'

'I've never seen them. I don't know anything about them,' said Jan. 'If I did, I wouldn't tell you.'

'What did the other boys pay you to stop the train?' asked Captain Greenwood.

'Nothing,' said Jan. 'Sometimes they gave me some of the food they took.'

'But you say you've never seen them.'

'They're clever,' said Jan. 'They leave the food in a hiding-place, in the forest.'

'But why do you steal food when you can get plenty from the army kitchens?' asked Captain Greenwood. 'It's just a bad habit, isn't it?'

'The Nazis stole everything from our country,' said Jan. 'Now it's our turn to steal from them.'

'But this is American food you've been stealing, not Nazi food. It's sent here to feed you and all the other refugees. If you steal it, you're robbing your own people. Do you think that's right or sensible?'

Jan began to cry. 'Edek is ill, and we are all hungry. I shall always steal if we are hungry.'

Captain Greenwood moved the papers around on his

desk. 'Edek Balicki,' he said, 'you can go. Jan, you will pay 200 marks or go to prison for seven days.'

Ruth and Jan talked together for a minute, then Ruth said, 'Jan says he'll go to prison. We don't have enough money to pay the 200 marks.'

'We're saving our money to buy some boots for Edek,' said Bronia.

'It isn't long, Jan, and you'll be looked after,' said Captain Greenwood, kindly. 'When you come out, stay with that mother – perhaps she'll be able to teach you not to steal. And remind her to send me a postcard when you get to Switzerland.'

9
The Bavarian farmer

It was early on a July morning when a Bavarian farmer pulled open the door of his barn. He stared into the dark building, remembering the noises he had heard. It was so quiet that he began to wonder if he had made a mistake. Suddenly, a potato flew out and hit him on the neck!

'Come out!' he shouted.

Ruth appeared, followed by Edek and Bronia.

'We only stayed here last night,' explained Ruth. 'We haven't done any harm to your barn.'

Another potato hit the farmer's shirt. 'No harm!' he shouted. 'I suppose that was a birthday present!'

Bronia laughed and Edek smiled, but Ruth was angry.

Another potato hit the farmer's shirt.

'When will you grow up, you silly boy!' she said, pulling Jan out of the barn. 'Say you're sorry.'

'Sorry,' Jan said to the farmer.

'Now perhaps you'll tell me what you're doing here,' said the farmer, looking at Edek.

Edek explained who they were and where they were

going. 'It was after dark when we arrived last night,' he said. 'We didn't want to wake you up. But we'll pay you for using your barn by doing a day's work.'

'Of course,' said the farmer. 'And if I'm not happy with that, I'll give you to the Burgomaster.'

'What's a Burgomaster?' asked Bronia.

'He's an important town official who will be very interested in you,' said the farmer. 'You're Poles, aren't you? Well, there's an order saying all Poles must be sent back to Poland now. It's the Burgomaster's job to see that this order is obeyed.'

'We've just come from Poland,' said Ruth. 'We're not going back again.'

'We're going to Switzerland to find our father and mother,' said Bronia.

'If the government decides that you must go back, then back you will go,' said the farmer. 'And throwing potatoes won't save you! Now come inside and have a bit of breakfast.'

Inside the farmhouse, on the kitchen table, was coffee and fresh bread.

'Emma!' called the farmer. 'We have four visitors from Poland. Ruth, Edek, Jan and Bronia. This is Frau Wolff, my wife.'

A large, comfortable-looking lady shook hands with each of them. Then she went to fetch more bread and coffee. She could speak Polish better than her husband, and conversation became easier.

'How did you get that dirt on your shirt?' Frau Wolff asked her husband, looking at the place where the potato had hit him.

'It was a present from Poland,' replied the farmer, smiling at Jan. And they all laughed so much that they almost knocked over the coffee.

'Eat all you can,' said Frau Wolff, putting more bread on the table.

'We get lots of refugees coming through here,' said the farmer, drinking his coffee. 'You're not the first ones I've found in my barn, but they have to work for their food. So don't think you're going to get a holiday with me! We'll start work right after breakfast.'

'Let them rest today, Kurt,' said his wife.

The farmer hit the table with his hand. 'I don't believe in making things easy for people,' he said. 'No, they'll start now. Ruth and Jan can come to the field, Bronia can feed the chickens, Edek can—'

'Edek will stay in the kitchen and help me,' said his wife. 'He's not strong enough to work outside.'

And the look she gave her husband made it clear that she didn't want any arguments.

Kurt Wolff's farm was high up in the Bavarian hills, not far from Czechoslovakia. There were trees right to the top of the hills, and between the hills was the River Falken.

A few kilometres away was the village of Boding, where each day the Burgomaster received his orders from the

American soldiers who were living there. His orders were to send all the Polish and Ukrainian refugees back home in American army lorries.

Most of the refugees were glad to go home, but others had reasons for not returning. Ruth and her family did not want to return, so they had to keep out of the Burgomaster's sight.

Jan liked living on the farm. He said it was as good as his week in prison, which he had enjoyed very much! He became friendly with an old dog named Ludwig. Until Jan arrived on the farm, Ludwig just lay in the sun doing nothing. Now he followed Jan everywhere.

One day, when they were in the kitchen, Ruth looked at a photograph of a young man which was on the shelf.

'Who is that?' she asked.

'That's my son,' said Frau Wolff quietly.

'You didn't say that you had children,' said Edek.

'We haven't,' said Frau Wolff. 'Hans was killed in North Africa. Rudolf, my younger son, died while he was fighting to keep the Russians out of Warsaw.'

'Was he in General Model's army?' asked Edek.

'Yes,' said Frau Wolff.

'Perhaps we saw him,' said Jan, looking closely at the photo. 'They all wore uniforms like that, and used to hide in the ruins to shoot at us. We hated them.'

'Some of the Germans were nice in the early days of the war,' said Ruth.

Jan stared at Frau Wolff, then looked back at the photo.

45

How could these friendly people have sons who had been German soldiers? He did not understand it.

'You and I should be enemies,' he said to the farmer.

'The only enemy you have,' said the farmer, 'is the Burgomaster, and he hasn't given you any trouble yet.'

'Rudolf loved Ludwig the way you do,' Frau Wolff told Jan. 'The dog became quiet and unhappy when Rudolf went away, but now you've come he's as happy as he used to be. You're like Rudolf in other ways, too.'

'Oh,' said Jan.

'He was sent to Warsaw to kill us,' said Ruth. 'I don't

'Rudolf loved Ludwig the way you do,' Frau Wolff told Jan.

suppose he wanted to very much. If he were here now, he would be as friendly as you are, Frau Wolff. It all seems so stupid.'

'You'd like to be our mother, wouldn't you, Frau Wolff?' said Bronia.

'Yes, my dear, I'd like to have you all. But you have your own mother and we must help you to find her.' She turned to Jan. 'You have no mother, Jan. Would you like to stay here?'

'Yes, I would, because of Ludwig. But I'd rather go with Ruth. And the sword won't let me stay here.'

'What sword?' said Frau Wolff.

Jan fetched it from his box, and explained how Joseph Balicki had given it to him, long ago; and how it now helped them to go on whenever they felt without hope.

He put it on the shelf next to the photo of Rudolf.

It shone brightly in the sunlight from the window.

10
The Burgomaster

Next day, Jan and Edek were working in the fields when a car went past on the road, throwing up a cloud of dust behind it. It was travelling very fast, and disappeared behind some trees. A moment later, there was a crash, followed by a shout.

'It's hit a tree,' said Jan.

'We'll have to go and help,' said Edek. 'The driver may be hurt.'

'No. You don't know who it is, Edek. Come back!'

But Edek was already running across the field.

The car had hit a tree and a man was getting out. There was blood on his head.

'Are you all right?' said Edek, in German.

'Yes, yes,' said the man. 'The car isn't badly damaged. Can you help me push it back on to the road?'

'I'll try,' said Edek. He guessed this man was the Burgomaster, but it did not worry him. Edek's German was good enough for the man not to guess he was Polish.

'Are you working for Kurt Wolff?' the man asked.

'Yes, he uses extra help at this time of the year.'

Suddenly, a small stone dropped out of a tree at Edek's feet. Edek looked up and saw Jan high among the branches, making signs at him.

'Where do you come from?' asked the man, as they pushed the car.

'The north,' said Edek.

'Oh. I thought you were a refugee.'

Edek began to cough. Pushing the car was hard for him, and the man realized this.

'I'm sorry,' said the man. 'You're not strong enough to do this. Perhaps the boy in the tree can help.'

Edek was surprised that the man knew Jan was there. 'It's my brother,' he said. 'Come down, Franz.'

After a moment, Jan dropped to the ground.

'So you come from the north, Franz?' said the man.

Jan did not answer. He could not speak German.

'He – he can't hear or speak,' said Edek.

They pushed the car back on to the road and the man was getting ready to drive off. Suddenly, Bronia appeared and spoke to them in Polish. Edek quickly replied in German, but the man said nothing about it.

'Thank you for your help,' he said. Then he got into the car and drove away.

'I think you're both stupid!' said Jan.

'Why did you climb into that tree?' said Edek.

'To warn you that it was the Burgomaster.'

'I already knew that,' said Edek. 'Anyway, I think everything will be all right.'

'Then you *are* stupid,' said Jan.

The next day the Burgomaster came to see the farmer.

'All Polish and Ukrainian refugees must be sent home by tomorrow. You're hiding Polish children here.' And the Burgomaster told him what had happened the day before. 'They must go home, like the rest,' he said.

'Their parents are in Switzerland, and they want to find them,' said the farmer.

The Burgomaster laughed. 'I've heard that story before. Anyone in trouble at home always tries to get to France or Switzerland. But the Swiss won't have them, unless the children can prove that one parent is alive and already in the country.'

The farmer took the silver sword from the shelf and told the Burgomaster its story. The Burgomaster laughed again.

'That's no proof. The mother's either dead or back in Poland now, and there's not a chance in a thousand that the father got through Germany alive.'

'I know he's alive,' said Edek, who had just come into the room. 'I know it in my heart.' He took the sword from the Burgomaster and put it back on the shelf.

The Burgomaster shook hands with him. 'Thank you for what you did for me yesterday,' he said. 'Where did you learn to speak German so well?'

Edek explained how he had been a prisoner during the war.

'You must hate us,' said the Burgomaster.

'I hate the Nazis who took our Mother and Father away, and destroyed our home and our city,' said Edek. 'But not all Germans are like that.'

Just then, Ruth came in with Bronia, Jan and Ludwig.

'A lorry will come for you tomorrow at twelve o'clock, midday,' said the Burgomaster. 'I shall expect you to be ready. Please don't try to escape. There is only one road, and there are American guards on it. There are guards in the forests, too.'

He looked tired.

'I warn you again, do not try to escape,' he said.

It was late that afternoon when the farmer remembered something.

'The canoes!' he said.

'What canoes?' said Ruth.

The farmer fetched them, together with three paddles. 'They belonged to my sons,' he said. 'Have you ever paddled canoes?'

'Yes,' replied Edek and Ruth together.

'There are only two difficult places on the River Falken,' said the farmer. 'The rapids, ten kilometres below the village, and the place where it joins the River Danube. But if you stay in the middle of the river, you'll be all right. It's your only chance to escape.'

The farmer fetched the canoes, together with three paddles.

So at three o'clock in the morning, two canoes and four sleepy children were taken down to the river. Frau Wolff gave them some food as the farmer put the canoes into the water.

'Say goodbye to Ludwig for me,' said Jan. 'I shall miss him very much.'

'Ludwig's in the forest somewhere,' said Bronia. 'I heard him.'

'Ludwig's asleep at home,' said Frau Wolff.

'Edek and Jan, you take the canoe with two seats,' said the farmer. 'We'll put the luggage in with you. Ruth and Bronia, you must fit into the one-seat canoe. It's only fifty kilometres to the Danube. Remember to be very quiet when you pass the village. There's no moon so I don't think anyone will see you. But if anyone shoots at you, lie as flat as you can.'

'Good luck!' said Frau Wolff.

'We can never thank you enough for all you've done for us,' said Ruth.

'I'll remember you for ever,' said Bronia.

The two boys waved with their paddles, and the farmer gave each canoe a gentle push out into the middle of the river.

'Goodbye,' he said. 'Good luck.'

Soon they were moving quickly away.

After a few minutes, Jan said, 'This canoe is very low in the water. There's something heavy in the front.'

Suddenly feeling alarmed, he put his hand under the

front of the canoe.

A wet nose touched his fingers.

'It's Ludwig!' said Jan, happily.

11
Dangerous water

The hills moved by in the darkness. For a moment, the moon appeared from behind a cloud and the water became like a sheet of silver.

'Go away, moon,' said Ruth. 'Don't come out again until we've passed the village.'

The two canoes moved quickly on.

Again the moon appeared, choosing the wrong moment because they were now passing by the village. Ruth could see the shadows of the houses, and the refugee lorries that were parked in rows.

'Look out for the bridge,' said Edek.

He and Jan moved ahead and went under the middle arch of the bridge. Ruth followed, aiming for the right-hand arch. But the canoe went into the slow-moving, shallow part of the river.

The water was noisy and Ruth did not hear feet walking across the bridge, but she saw a man's shadow on the water.

'The water's coming in,' said Bronia. 'I can feel it under me.'

There was a sudden shout above them. A man began to wave. Ruth could not understand what he was saying, but then he put a leg over the side of the bridge – and dropped down into the shallow water.

He was an American soldier.

Ruth tried to pull away, but the man caught her paddle and held on to it. Ruth pulled hard, but the man held on to the paddle. She pulled and turned the paddle sharply, but still he held on. Then she let go of the paddle, and the soldier fell backwards as the canoe was carried under the bridge and back into the fast-moving water.

Ruth pulled hard, but the soldier held on to the paddle.

Someone was shooting at them now, from the bridge. Ruth pushed Bronia's head down and looked around for the other canoe. Then the moon went behind a cloud and the dark night closed round her. The shooting stopped but Ruth had no paddle now and the water carried them wherever it wanted.

'Edek! Jan!' shouted Ruth.

They went round a bend and were pushed towards the right-hand side of the river. The water was quieter here, but the bottom of the canoe touched the ground and stopped. Ruth put her hand over the side and tried to push the canoe off the ground, but it didn't move. The sky began to get lighter and she saw rocks in the water.

'We'll have to get out and push,' she said.

Ruth and Bronia got out of the canoe – and it immediately began to move again. Ruth guided it towards a large rock, then pulled it up on to some small dry stones that stood above the water. She lifted Bronia on to the rock.

'We must wait here until daylight,' she said.

They waited until the shadows of the night disappeared, and they could see the whole of the river. It was white and broken with hidden rocks in the middle, and there were more rocks in the shallow parts on each side.

There was no sign of Jan and Edek anywhere, and both girls felt lonely and frightened. Then Bronia saw something in the water, near the rock she was sitting on.

'It's our paddle!' she shouted. 'The water carried it down to us! What good luck! Now we can go on.'

Soon, Ruth could see the rapids ahead of them, and she knew this was the most dangerous part of the river. Here the water moved very fast, hurrying between large rocks, some of them as high as houses.

The noise filled their ears, and Bronia closed her eyes. But Ruth found she was almost too excited to be afraid. She threw her paddle from side to side, always turning away from the white, broken water where the sharp rocks lay hidden. It became a battle between her and the wild river. But a quick touch with the paddle at the right moment was enough to shoot them safely past each rock.

Then the river became wider, and once again there were trees on either side. The water slowed down, and Ruth realized that they had got through safely. She thought about Edek and Jan. Had they got through the rapids, too?

She lay back and watched the sky as Bronia slept. Then she herself became sleepy and closed her eyes.

She woke to find herself sitting in water. To her horror, she saw that the canoe had hit a rock in shallow water, and there was a large hole in the bottom. The hole was much too big to mend.

She woke Bronia. 'We'll have to leave the canoe and walk,' she said. Bronia looked alarmed. 'Don't worry. It can't be far to the Danube now.'

They walked through the trees to the place where the river joined the Danube at Falkenburg. There were no trees here, only green fields, a dusty road, and a good view of the river. Ruth looked up and down it, hoping to see Jan and Edek.

There was an unfinished haystack in one field. Ruth did not know that Jan and Edek had waited in the field all morning, hoping to see Ruth's canoe come down the river. They had become tired and had climbed up on to the haystack. First Jan went to sleep while Edek watched the river, then Jan watched while Edek slept.

Now, Ruth was passing the haystack when a half-eaten apple hit her on the shoulder. Then she heard a dog, and found Ludwig jumping round her ankles.

'Where have you been?' Jan's voice shouted from the top of the haystack. 'We thought you'd got into trouble on the rapids.'

'Where have you been?' Jan shouted from the haystack.

He pushed the sleeping Edek, and the boy dropped to the ground in front of Bronia. They were all pleased to see each other again, and told their stories.

'We lost our canoe on some rocks, too,' said Edek.

A hundred metres away, American lorries crowded with Polish refugees moved along a dusty road. But the children were too busy laughing and talking even to notice them.

12
Missing

They walked into Falkenburg, crossed the Danube, then a lorry took them some way along the road to Switzerland. After this, there was more walking. Three days later, tired but happy, they were camping beside the road.

'Only a hundred and thirty kilometres to Lake Constance,' said Ruth, looking for some dry grass for Bronia to lie in.

'Is Lake Constance in Switzerland?' asked Bronia, sleepily.

'Switzerland is on the far side of the lake. Lie down here, Bronia. The grass is nice and thick.'

'Will Mother be waiting for us?' asked Bronia.

'Perhaps she will,' said Ruth. And in the half-light of the evening, nobody noticed that her eyes were wet with tears.

Jan's wooden box was one of the things they had saved from the canoes. He had been too busy to think about it before, but tonight he opened it to make sure everything was safe. Suddenly, he jumped up.

'The sword's missing!' he said. 'Someone's stolen it!'

58

'Nobody would do that,' said Ruth. 'Did you leave it at the farm?'

Jan thought for a moment. 'Yes, and I'm going back for it.'

He began to walk away but Ruth stopped him. 'Don't be stupid. The Wolffs are honest people. They'll look after it until we send for it.'

Just then, Edek began coughing. He had been coughing a lot since the river adventure, and the pain in his chest was getting worse. Ruth was worried when she saw how ill he looked. She made him lie down, then covered him with a blanket.

'Light a fire, Jan,' said Ruth. 'It will help Edek to sleep.' It was a warm night and they did not need a fire, but Ruth wanted to give Jan something to do. When the fire was burning and the other three were sleeping, she stayed awake to make sure that Jan didn't run off.

At midnight, a voice called her name. It was Edek.

'I thought you were asleep,' said Ruth.

'I can't sleep . . . The pain is too bad,' said Edek. 'I can't . . . walk any more.'

'We'll find a lorry to ride in,' said Ruth. 'It's only a hundred and thirty kilometres.'

'There's no traffic going that way,' said Edek.

Ruth talked to him quietly until he went to sleep again, but she was too worried about her brother to sleep herself. 'If we don't reach Switzerland soon,' she thought, 'he may not live.'

An hour later, she heard another voice. It was Jan. 'Ruth, may I have Edek's shoes when he dies?'

'He's not going to die,' said Ruth, making herself speak calmly.

'He will if I don't have my sword,' said Jan. 'And we'll never find your father, either.'

Ruth almost believed him. It was true that they had been very fortunate while they had the sword. And now Edek was very ill. But all she said was, 'Go to sleep, Jan. Everything will be all right.'

But after a while, Ruth could not keep awake any longer. When she woke in the morning, Jan and Ludwig had both gone. And Edek's face looked so white that at first Ruth was afraid he was dead. For a few moments, Ruth felt desperately alone.

'Jan can look after himself,' said Bronia, when she discovered that he had gone.

'He forgets that we may need him to look after *us*,' said Ruth.

The sun shone on to Edek's face and woke him. He was too ill to notice that Jan and Ludwig were missing.

'What's wrong with Edek?' asked Bronia.

'I expect it's the hot sun,' said Ruth.

Edek could only walk very slowly, with Ruth holding his arm. After less than a kilometre he had to stop and sit down on the road.

'I can't go on,' he said, his voice a whisper.

Ruth pulled him out of the sun. 'Stay by the road,

'I can't go on,' Edek said, his voice a whisper.

Bronia,' she said. 'Stop the first person who passes.'

Half an hour later, a lorry came along. The driver saw Bronia and stopped. She called to him in Polish, and he smiled. He was an American soldier, but he answered her in Polish.

'Have you come from Poland, too?' said Bronia.

'No, I'm from America, but my parents were Polish,' explained the driver. 'Joe Wolski's my name but call me Joe. Now, little lady, what's your trouble?'

They got in the front seat of the lorry beside Joe Wolski and went off along the road to Switzerland.

'What's in the back of your lorry?' asked Bronia, hearing a noise.

'A wild animal,' said Joe.

'Jan likes animals,' said Bronia. And she told him how Jan had run away.

Joe smiled. 'I knew a boy who ran away like Jan,' he said. 'I went to sleep in the back of my lorry, and when I woke up in the morning, there he was beside me! He had climbed in during the night. I woke him up and asked him what he was doing. He said he was going north, and asked me to take him to a village – I've forgotten the name. Now, I *was* going north, but when I heard his story, I decided not to go. I told him he was wrong to leave his family alone, but he shouted and screamed and kicked me. So what did I do? I tied him up and left him in the back of the lorry.'

Bronia was going to ask a question when she heard a dog barking in the back of the lorry.

'That must be the wild animal,' said Joe. 'Do you want to see it?' He stopped by the side of the road and Ruth and Bronia followed him round to the back of the lorry. He lifted them up – and there on the floor was Jan! His mouth was covered and his hands and feet were tied up. Ludwig was standing beside him.

Joe untied Jan. 'How are you feeling?' he asked, with a smile.

Jan's answer was to kick at Joe.

'You see?' said Joe. 'I told you there was a wild animal in the back of my lorry. And here he is!'

'Please, Jan! Stop kicking,' begged Ruth. But he didn't stop.

Joe gave him some chocolate. 'Does this make you feel better?' said the soldier.

Jan threw the chocolate back at Joe.

'Oh dear, I'll have to tie him up again,' said Joe.

So Jan travelled the rest of the way to Lake Constance tied up in the back of the lorry. It was a rough road and the lorry made a lot of noise.

But Jan made a lot more.

13
The storm

There was a refugee camp near Lake Constance and Joe took the children there. The camp official wanted to put Edek into the hospital and to send the others away, but Ruth would not allow this.

But the camp official would not let the children go across the lake to Switzerland without proof that one of their parents was already there. Ruth did not know if her father was in Switzerland, and she could not remember the address of her mother's parents in Basel.

'Perhaps the sword can help us prove who we are,' she thought, and she wrote to the farmer asking him to send it to her.

Ruth was feeling sad when she said goodbye to Joe. They had come a long way, and now they could *see* Switzerland, but reaching it seemed harder than before.

'Thank you for being so kind, Joe,' she said.

From Warsaw to Switzerland – a long journey

'Don't call me kind,' said Joe. 'There are problems everywhere. I just want to help. I want to show people that you can't learn everything about life from a hole in a bombed cellar. Sometimes good things *do* happen to people.' He shook Ruth's hand. 'And this is going to be one of those times.'

The hot days went by slowly. There was thunder in the air, but the black clouds held back their rain. They seemed to be saving it for some special but terrible day.

Ruth thought about borrowing a small boat and crossing the lake by themselves, but Edek's illness kept him in bed for most of the day. The camp official sent the information that Ruth gave him to the I.T.S. (International Tracing Service). But his letter to Basel about her mother's parents had not been answered. And Ruth had received no reply from the farmer about the sword.

Then one day, in late August, the camp official asked Ruth to come and see him. 'Can you describe that sword that you told me about?' he said.

Ruth did this, and once again told the story of its adventures. A smile appeared on the official's face.

'Ruth, you're the luckiest girl in Europe,' he said.

He took two letters – and the sword – from his desk.

One letter was from the farmer. The other was from Ruth's father. Both were addressed to the I.T.S. The farmer's letter told some of the story of the family, and gave details of their plans for getting to Switzerland. He had found the sword the day after the children had left, and

65

immediately sent it to the I.T.S. with the letter. (Ruth's letter to him had got lost. It would be many months before she would get a reply to it.)

The letter from Ruth's father had a January date on it. In it, he described the children and when he had last seen them. He also wrote about his escape from the German prison, how he met Jan and gave him the sword, and about his long journey to Switzerland.

'I received this information two days ago,' said the camp official. 'I wrote to your father, and his reply came today. He lives in Appenzell, on the other side of the lake. He will collect all of you at Meersburg tomorrow, by the afternoon boat.'

The next morning, Joseph Balicki tried to speak to Ruth on the phone, but the telephone line was bad and she could not hear him. Then there was silence. What was he trying to tell her? she wondered.

The children waited by the lake for the Swiss boat to come and fetch them. They were so excited that they did not see the dark clouds getting thicker above them. Only Ludwig was unhappy, but nobody noticed this.

'Let's go to that hill over there,' said Jan. 'We'll have a better view of the lake.'

'It means we have to cross this stream,' said Ruth.

'It's a very small stream,' said Jan.

It was true. There had been very little rain that summer and it was easy to jump from rock to rock and get across the shallow water without getting their feet wet.

'I'll stay on this side,' said Edek, who was feeling tired.

'Good idea,' said Ruth. 'Sit on that rock.'

But when she was on the other side of the stream, she called back to him. 'Edek! There's a boat that's been pulled up on the ground behind you. You can get inside it, if it rains.'

And at that moment, it *did* begin to rain. Edek laughed and got inside the boat.

There was the sound of thunder from the Swiss mountains. Then lightning appeared through the clouds, and more thunder followed it. Suddenly, the clouds seemed to open up and a great sheet of rain fell out of the sky. In just a few seconds, Ruth, Jan and Bronia were wet through to their skins, and there was water up to their ankles.

It was impossible to see through the heavy rain. Ruth reached for Bronia's hand, and found it. She tried to find Jan's, but he was trying to calm Ludwig. She got hold of his shirt, but he pulled away.

'We must go back to Edek!' shouted Ruth.

It was not so easy to do. She fell over a broken tree branch, then tried to feel her way along the edge of the lake. It was some time before she realized she was going the wrong way. She went back again. But the quiet little stream was now a wide river, carrying bits of wood and whole trees in its wild, fast-moving water.

'Edek! Edek!' she cried. 'We'll never get across!'

Then the rain became lighter and she could see across the

river. 'Edek must be on the other side,' she thought.

But Edek was not there. Nor was the boat.

The water was all around them, rising up above their knees. Ruth pulled Bronia on to some ground which the water had not yet reached.

'Where's Jan gone?' shouted Bronia.

'I don't care where he's gone!' Ruth shouted back. 'I told him to stay with us, but he went after Ludwig. Edek! Edek!' Pushing wet hair away from her eyes, she looked out across the lake. If Edek was still in the boat, perhaps the water had carried him out there, she thought. But she could not see the boat anywhere.

'Jan's on the cliff behind us,' said Bronia.

Ruth turned. 'Can you see him from there, Jan?' she shouted.

'He jumped out of my arms and ran away,' called Jan. He was looking towards the land, not the lake.

'I mean Edek – can you see his boat?'

But Jan didn't answer. He was thinking of Ludwig.

'I think I can see Edek's boat in the middle of the lake!' shouted Bronia.

Ruth looked again. She saw it for a moment – and then it disappeared. But Ruth was sure it had been Edek's boat, and that he had been in it.

Bronia was the first to see the empty rowing boat, as it was carried past them by the river. She shouted to Ruth, who jumped towards it, catching the side. Jan came to help her.

'Go away and look for your dog!' Ruth told him. 'You

don't care about Edek. I hate you!'

But Jan held on to the boat and together they pulled it to the side of the river. There was one oar and some rope inside the boat.

'Go after your dog!' Ruth shouted to Jan. 'Look, there's Ludwig up by the road. Run after him and don't come back. Bronia and I can save Edek without you.'

The two girls jumped into the boat. Jan was staring at the dog. He wanted to run after the animal, but Ruth's words had hurt him. He looked back at her brave face, and he knew what he had to do. He had lost Ludwig, but he could not lose Ruth.

'Go after your dog!' Ruth shouted. 'And don't come back.'

His wooden box was under his arm. He threw it into the boat and jumped in after it. Then he put the oar into the water and began to row.

In that moment, Jan began to grow up.

14
Safe!

It was dark when Ruth opened her eyes. Someone was lifting her.

'It's a girl,' a man's voice said. 'How are you feeling? We nearly went into you in the dark.'

She did not understand him, and tried to speak, but no words came. Then everything went black again.

The next time Ruth woke up, she called out, 'Edek! Bronia! Jan!' There were voices all round her, but she could not understand what they were saying. Then she heard another, deep voice. It said, 'Edek! Bronia! Jan!' like an echo. It was her father's voice!

Then her eyes closed again.

When she woke up again, he was beside her.

'You've been asleep a long time,' he said. 'Try to stay awake, and I'll show you something.' He lifted her from the bed she was resting on. 'Look down there.'

She looked down at a bed and saw Bronia's sleeping head among the blankets. Her father carried her to the next bed, and there was Edek's thin white face, also asleep.

'Is he breathing?' Ruth asked.

'Yes, he's breathing,' said Joseph. And he carried her away and showed her Jan.

The boy was sitting on the edge of a bed. 'You Balickis are no good at sailing. You can't manage without me. You use an oar like a soup spoon,' Jan told Ruth. 'And when a bit of water comes into the boat, you faint! I had to find Edek's boat and get ours across to it. I shouted to him to help, but he had fainted, too. So I pulled him into our boat, just before his went under the water.'

Joseph smiled at him. 'Now eat your food and stop talking,' he said to Jan.

Ruth put her arms round her father's neck. 'All three of them are safe!' she said, happily.

'Four,' said her father. 'Four of them. I tried to tell you over the phone, but you couldn't hear me.'

He opened a door to another room on the boat. There was a woman inside, and she had been waiting for the door to open. Her arms reached out to Ruth.

'Mother!' said Ruth. And she moved from her father's arms into those other arms.

'Mother was sitting with you when you were asleep,' Joseph said. 'She went away before you woke up. We didn't want to give you too many surprises at once.'

Someone knocked at the door, and Jan came in.

'Ruth, I wanted to tell you I haven't got my wooden box any more,' he said. 'It fell into the lake.'

'What about the silver sword?' said Ruth. 'Is that lost, too? I gave it back to you, I know I did.'

Jan pulled open his shirt. And there was the silver sword, tied to a thin piece of rope round his neck. 'I knew if I kept the sword safe,' he said to Joseph, 'we would find you again.'

He untied the sword and gave it to Ruth's mother.

'Joseph gave it to me, but it's yours now,' he said. 'You can keep it for ever if you'll be my mother.'

*   *   *

An international children's village was built in Appenzell. It was the first village like this in the world. Each nation had its own house, where sixteen children who had lost their parents could live. There they could grow up with the children of the house-parents.

Joseph Balicki and his wife became the house-parents of the Polish house.

Bronia grew up a happy child, drawing pictures and playing with the other children. At first, her drawings were full of ruined buildings, soldiers and field kitchens. But slowly they changed to pictures of happier things – the lake and the Swiss mountains.

Edek was sent to a hospital, and at first the doctors were afraid he was going to die. But Edek lived and, after eighteen months, returned to his family. Six months of Swiss mountain air made him fully well, and then he went to study in Zurich.

The I.T.S. could find out nothing about Jan's parents, so he became a Balicki. Margrit Balicki loved him as much as she loved her own children, but Ruth was the only person who could manage him. She knew that the way to his heart was through animals, and she took him to the farms near the village where the farmers soon discovered that Jan could do almost anything with a sick animal. So in time, even the wild Jan grew up and learned to behave well.

At the beginning, Ruth found the new life more difficult than the others. She had been clever and brave and had looked after Edek, Bronia and Jan like a mother. But she had grown up too quickly, and at first she behaved like a young child, not wanting to leave her mother, and following Margrit Balicki everywhere. But slowly Ruth became better, and in 1947 she went to Zurich university. Four years later, then a teacher, she married a young Frenchman who had come to work in the children's village. When a second French house was built, Ruth and her husband became house-parents. They may still be there.

And not far away, in the Polish house, Margrit Balicki keeps something very special, in its own special box.

The silver sword.

GLOSSARY

attic   a room at the top of a house, under the roof

camp   a place for people to live for a short time

cart   a kind of open 'car' on wheels, usually pulled by horses

cellar   a room under the ground in a house

cough   to send out air from the mouth and throat in a noisy way

Council   a group of people who are chosen to work together and to decide things for other people

court-room   a place where judges, lawyers, etc. listen to law cases

elastic   a kind of 'string' that gets longer when you pull it

faint   to fall down suddenly because you are weak or ill

grow up   to become an adult; to change from a child to a man or woman

look after   to take care of someone or something

nail   a small piece of metal with a sharp end, used to fix things together

Nazis   members of the German National Socialist Party, who controlled Germany under their leader, Hitler

rapids   part of a river where the water moves very fast

refugee   someone who is running away from war or danger and trying to find a new, safe home

ruin   a building which is almost destroyed and is falling down

ruined   almost destroyed

silly   not sensible; stupid

zone   (in this story) a part of a country which is controlled by soldiers from another country

The Silver Sword

ACTIVITIES

Before Reading

1 Read the back cover and the story introduction on the first page of the book. Are these sentences true (T) or false (F)?

1 Jan stole the silver sword from Mr Balicki.
2 Life in Warsaw is difficult and dangerous for the children.
3 The children's home is used as a prison camp.
4 The children want to go to Switzerland because they hope their parents are there.
5 Jan keeps the silver sword because he thinks it is lucky.

2 What is going to happen in the story? Can you guess? For each sentence, circle Y (Yes) or N (No).

1 Jan will go to prison. Y/N
2 Mr Balicki will see the silver sword again. Y/N
3 One of the children dies on the journey. Y/N
4 The children will find both of their parents. Y/N
5 Jan will find his family again. Y/N

3 What do you know about the time and place of this story? Choose the correct words to complete this passage.

The Second World War began in *1939 / 1940* and ended in *1943 / 1945*. The children lived in Poland, in *eastern / western* Europe. To get to Switzerland, they had to go *west / east* to Germany, and then *north / south* to Switzerland.

ACTIVITIES

While Reading

Read Chapters 1 to 3. Choose the best question-word for these questions, and then answer them.

Where / How / What / Why

1 . . . did Joseph escape from the prison?
2 . . . did Joseph get to the other side of the valley?
3 . . . did the prison bell ring?
4 . . . happened to Joseph's wife?
5 . . . did the Nazis destroy Joseph's home with a bomb?
6 . . . did Joseph ask Jan to do if he ever met his children?
7 . . . did Jan take Joseph that night?

Read Chapters 4 and 5. Are these sentences true (T) or false (F)? Rewrite the false ones with the correct information.

1 The children climbed onto the roof and escaped before the bombs exploded.
2 The children stole food from anyone.
3 Ruth began a school for homeless children.
4 Edek was taken away by the secret police.
5 Ruth and Bronia lived in the forest all the time.
6 Ruth asked the Russian officer to find her parents.
7 Jan did not hate Russian soldiers.
8 Ruth only found out about the silver sword because Ivan broke Jan's wooden box and the sword fell out.

Before you read Chapter 6, can you guess what Jan and Ruth will decide to do?

1 Jan, Ruth and Bronia will look for Edek, and then for their parents.
2 Jan will go to Switzerland to find Mr Balicki.
3 Jan will stay with Bronia in Warsaw while Ruth goes to look for Edek and her parents.

Read Chapters 6 to 8. Here are some untrue sentences about them. Change them into true sentences.

1 Edek was waiting for them at the Warthe camp.
2 When the fight at the field kitchen finished, Ruth was holding Jan's hand.
3 Jan believed Edek's story about hiding under a train.
4 In Berlin the children stayed in an old hospital.
5 Edek was helping Jan to steal food from the trains.
6 The American Captain told Jan he had been stealing Nazi food sent to feed the soldiers.
7 Jan went to prison although the children had enough money to pay the 200 marks.

Read Chapters 9 and 10. Who said these words, and to whom? Who, or what, were they talking about?

1 'I suppose that was a birthday present!'
2 'He's not strong enough to work outside.'
3 'You and I should be enemies.'
4 'We must help you to find her.'

5 'He – he can't hear or speak.'
6 'They must go home, like the rest.'
7 'I know he's alive. I know it in my heart.'
8 'It's your only chance to escape.'

Read Chapters 11 to 13, and answer these questions.

1 How did Ruth get away from the American soldier?
2 What piece of good luck did the girls have after the bridge?
3 What had happened to the silver sword?
4 Why was Ruth so worried at their camp by the road side?
5 Why did Jan run away in the night?
6 Why did Joe tie Jan up?
7 Why did the camp official finally allow the children to go across the lake to Switzerland?
8 What happened to Edek in the storm?
9 Why didn't Ruth want Jan to come in the rowing boat?

Before you read Chapter 14, can you guess how the story will end? Circle Y (Yes) or N (No) for each sentence.

1 The four children are rescued from the lake. Y/N
2 Joseph Balicki is in Switzerland, but the children's mother is dead. Y/N
3 Edek is very ill, and dies some time later. Y/N
4 Jan finds his parents and goes to live with them. Y/N
5 Ruth finds it more difficult than the others to get used to their new life. Y/N
6 Jan keeps the silver sword to bring him luck. Y/N

After Reading

1 **Here is the conversation between Joe Wolski and Jan when they first met. Put it into the correct order and write in the speakers' names. Joe speaks first (number 5).**

1 _____ 'Well, I was with my family till yesterday. But they didn't want me to go back to Boding, so I ran away.'

2 _____ 'And where are you going?'

3 _____ 'Ow! What are you doing? No! Let me go!'

4 _____ 'Because Edek's sick, and Ruth wanted me to help them. But I've *got* to go to Boding.'

5 _____ 'Hello, young man! What are you doing in my lorry?'

6 _____ 'Right. You can just stay here now, nice and quiet. I *was* going to drive north, but I've now decided we'll go south – to find your family.'

7 _____ 'Just a minute. You're rather young to be travelling by yourself, aren't you?'

8 _____ 'I needed somewhere to sleep, so I climbed in here while you were sleeping. But I've got to go now.'

9 _____ 'If they need your help, young man, you're wrong to leave them alone. You should be with them. So I think you should – Hey! There's no need to kick me!'

10 _____ 'Why didn't they want you to go?'

11 _____ 'North. I've left something in a village called Boding. Are you going north? Can you take me there?'

2 Here are some passages from the diaries of four of the characters in the story. Complete them with words from the list, and then say who wrote each one, and when.

away, been, before, better, canoes, cellar, cockerel, escape, even, everyone, idea, knife, luck, miserable, must, news, reminds, safely, secret, started, until, wild, worse

1 I've _____ living here for a week now, and I've decided to stay. _____ wants to look in my box, but they'd _____ look out! The sword is my _____, and I'm not going to show it to anyone. If I keep it, I know it will bring me _____.

2 What a strange day! I'd just arrived at the _____ with chocolate and good _____ for the girls, when suddenly this _____ boy was trying to put a _____ in my neck and a _____ was biting my ankles! Luckily, nobody was hurt, but the boy's box got broken. Then Ruth _____crying! I had no _____ what it was all about!

3 I wish they could stay. Jan _____ me so much of Rudolf. _____ Ludwig agrees! But I know they must leave tonight, _____ the Burgomaster can take them _____. I just hope they'll reach the Danube _____ in those old _____ . . .

4 This _____ be the most _____ place in the world. If the food was any _____, and the work was any harder, we'd all die. Tonight I'm going to try again to _____. And this time I won't stop _____ I'm back in Warsaw with Ruth and Bronia.

3 There are 14 words from the story hidden in this word search. Find the words, and draw a line through them. The first and last letters of each word are given below, and the words go from left to right, and from top to bottom.

a_____h   c_____e   m_____s   r_____e   s_____l

b_____n   c_____r   p_____e   r_____e   z_____e

c_____p   l_____y   r_____s   r_____n

J	O	C	A	M	P	S	E	P	H
S	G	B	A	R	N	R	A	L	V
I	Z	O	N	E	E	U	R	O	I
G	A	T	T	O	M	I	O	R	E
N	R	B	U	T	I	N	P	R	C
A	C	E	L	L	A	R	E	Y	A
L	H	P	A	D	D	L	E	T	N
S	Y	R	I	F	L	E	O	U	O
R	A	P	I	D	S	R	S	N	E
O	W	M	A	T	T	R	E	S	S

Now write down all the letters that don't have a line through them, beginning with the first line and going across each line to the end. You should have thirty letters, which will make a sentence of nine words.

1 What is the sentence?

2 Who said it, and to whom?

3 What was he holding in his hands?

4 **Complete this letter from Ruth to the Wolffs. Use as many words as you like.**

My dear friends,
At last we have arrived at a camp near Lake Constance. The journey in the canoes was quite difficult for Bronia and me. When we passed the village, an American soldier _____. We got away from him when _____. Later we found our paddle, and went down the river to Falkenburg. There we found _____.

Edek became very ill and I was worried that _____. Luckily, a soldier called Joe Wolski _____.

Now we want to go to Switzerland – but first we have to _____. Jan thinks that he _____. Could you send it to us? Then perhaps the camp official _____.

Thank you so much for _____. We will _____.
Love from Ruth

5 **Do you agree (A) or disagree (D) with the following statements? Explain why.**

1 In wartime it is all right to steal food from the enemy, but not from your own people.
2 It is always all right to steal food if you have no food or money.
3 In wartime you have to look after yourself first.
4 In wartime people have to help each other more than ever.
5 'Soldier' or 'German' are just names, and the person inside is more important than the name outside.

ABOUT THE AUTHOR

Ian Serraillier was born in London in 1912. He was educated in Brighton and Oxford, and then became a school teacher. From a very early age, however, he wanted to be a writer, and his first book was published in 1944. He went on to write many more books, including poems, plays, and stories, and with his wife, Anne Serraillier, he also edited a series of children's books. He died in 1994.

Most of Ian Serraillier's books were written for children, and he was a very good story teller – he knew how to make a story exciting and keep his readers interested. Some of his best books retell the great stories of the past, about heroes such as Jason, Hercules, and Beowulf. The Beowulf story is retold in verse, in his collection *The Windmill Book of Ballads* (1962). He also wrote adventure stories, including *There's No Escape* (1950) and *The Cave of Death* (1965).

His most famous book, however, is *The Silver Sword*, which is one of the most remarkable children's books published since World War II. The children – Ruth, Edek, Bronia, and Jan – were not real people themselves, but the book, Ian Serraillier said, had 'a basis in fact'. Before he wrote the story, he spent five years carefully studying the background, and the history and experiences of many refugees.

The Silver Sword was first published in 1956, and nearly half a century later it is still read and enjoyed by thousands of readers each year. It has been published in many translations, and has twice been made into a film for television.

ABOUT BOOKWORMS

OXFORD BOOKWORMS LIBRARY
Classics • True Stories • Fantasy & Horror • Human Interest
Crime & Mystery • Thriller & Adventure

The OXFORD BOOKWORMS LIBRARY offers a wide range of original and adapted stories, both classic and modern, which take learners from elementary to advanced level through six carefully graded language stages:

Stage 1 (400 headwords)	**Stage 4** (1400 headwords)
Stage 2 (700 headwords)	**Stage 5** (1800 headwords)
Stage 3 (1000 headwords)	**Stage 6** (2500 headwords)

More than fifty titles are also available on cassette, and there are many titles at Stages 1 to 4 which are specially recommended for younger learners. In addition to the introductions and activities in each Bookworm, resource material includes photocopiable test worksheets and Teacher's Handbooks, which contain advice on running a class library and using cassettes, and the answers for the activities in the books.

Several other series are linked to the OXFORD BOOKWORMS LIBRARY. They range from highly illustrated readers for young learners, to playscripts, non-fiction readers, and unsimplified texts for advanced learners.

Oxford Bookworms Starters	*Oxford Bookworms Factfiles*
Oxford Bookworms Playscripts	*Oxford Bookworms Collection*

Details of these series and a full list of all titles in the OXFORD BOOKWORMS LIBRARY can be found in the *Oxford English* catalogues. A selection of titles from the OXFORD BOOKWORMS LIBRARY can be found on the next pages.

Treasure Island

ROBERT LOUIS STEVENSON

Retold by John Escott

'Suddenly, there was a high voice screaming in the darkness: "Pieces of eight! Pieces of eight! Pieces of eight!" It was Long John Silver's parrot, Captain Flint! I turned to run . . .'

But young Jim Hawkins does not escape from the pirates this time. Will he and his friends find the treasure before the pirates do? Will they escape from the island, and sail back to England with a ship full of gold?

The Eagle of the Ninth

ROSEMARY SUTCLIFF

Retold by John Escott

In the second century AD, when the Ninth Roman Legion marched into the mists of northern Britain, not one man came back. Four thousand men disappeared, and the Eagle, the symbol of the Legion's honour, was lost.

Years later there is a story that the Eagle has been seen again. So Marcus Aquila, whose father disappeared with the Ninth, travels north, to find the Eagle and bring it back, and to learn how his father died. But the tribes of the north are wild and dangerous, and they hate the Romans . . .

BOOKWORMS • THRILLER & ADVENTURE • STAGE 4

Mr Midshipman Hornblower

C. S. FORESTER

Retold by Rosemary Border

Hornblower fired. There was a small cloud of smoke, but no bang. 'This is death,' he thought. 'My pistol was the unloaded one.'

But Horatio Hornblower does not die. He survives the duel with Simpson, learns to overcome his seasickness, and goes on to risk his life many times over. It is 1793, Britain is at war with France, and life on a sailing ship of war is hard and dangerous. But the hardest battles are fought by Hornblower within himself.

BOOKWORMS • THRILLER & ADVENTURE • STAGE 4

We Didn't Mean to Go to Sea

ARTHUR RANSOME

Retold by Ralph Mowat

The four Walker children never meant to go to sea. They had promised their mother they would stay safely in the harbour, and would be home on Friday in time for tea.

But there they are in someone else's boat, drifting out to sea in a thick fog. When the fog lifts, they can turn round and sail back to the harbour. But then comes the wind and the storm, driving them out even further across the cold North Sea . . .

Little Women

LOUISA MAY ALCOTT

Retold by John Escott

When Christmas comes for the four March girls, there is no money for expensive presents and they give away their Christmas breakfast to a poor family. But there are no happier girls in America than Meg, Jo, Beth, and Amy. They miss their father, of course, who is away at the Civil War, but they try hard to be good so that he will be proud of his 'little women' when he comes home.

This heart-warming story of family life has been popular for more than a hundred years.

Great Expectations

CHARLES DICKENS

Retold by Clare West

In a gloomy, neglected house Miss Havisham sits, as she has sat year after year, in a wedding dress and veil that were once white, and are now faded and yellow with age. Her face is like a death's head; her dark eyes burn with bitterness and hate. By her side sits a proud and beautiful girl, and in front of her, trembling with fear in his thick country boots, stands young Pip.

Miss Havisham stares at Pip coldly, and murmurs to the girl at her side: 'Break his heart, Estella. Break his heart!'